When OWEN's Mom Breathed Fire

PIJA LINDENBAUM

Translated by
Elisabeth Kallick Dyssegaard

R&S BOOKS

Stockholm   New York   London   Adelaide   Toronto

This is a boy. His name is Owen, and he almost always wears that dragon head. Owen's mom's name is Bea, and in the morning she goes completely crazy.

"Be careful with the milk," she screams. "And hurry up and eat your toast!"
Then Owen puts on his dragon head. It's nice and quiet inside.
Mom thinks there's something wrong with Owen's ears.
"We'll have to go to the doctor," she yells. "Now, where did I put the keys? I think I'm going insane. We're going to be late again!" And then they have to run to daycare.

One morning something very strange happens. Owen gets up
before Mom. But when he goes in to nudge her, he discovers
that she has turned into some sort of dragon.

"Are you okay?" asks Owen.

"More or less," says Mom.

"I'm hungry," says Owen. "And I have to go to daycare.
Come on, hurry up!"

But Mom has completely forgotten how to make breakfast.

Owen gets everything out.

"Here you go," he says. "We'll have toast with chocolate powder on it, and chocolate milk. And cornflakes with chocolate milk!"

"Hmm," says Mom. "Is that what we usually have?"

"Yep," says Owen. "Every day."

Mom says she can't remember a thing about what she does at work. So Owen calls her office.

"Hi, it's Owen. My mom can't come to work today. There's something in her ears."

Later they clear the table. Mom puts the milk in the hallway closet and the cornflakes on the toilet seat. The knobs on the dishwasher are complicated, so she licks the dishes clean instead and puts them in the cabinet.

Usually Mom makes the bed while Owen gets ready,
but today she falls asleep right on top of the covers.
"Oh, no," says Owen. "Something is definitely wrong.
We'll have to go to the hospital. Maybe the doctor will have
some anti-dragon medicine."

When they get outside, Mom livens up right away. A fat
beetle is creeping along the wall. She licks it up. Then her
coat pocket rings. Mom takes out her cell phone and
stomps on it.
"I don't like the way it rings all the time," she complains.
"Come on, let's go," says Owen, and takes Mom's hand. It feels
a bit rough. But this is still his mom.

The zoo is on the way to the hospital.

"Let's go in," Owen suggests. "I want to check out the pythons and the tigers."

"Animals get in free," says the lady at the window.

"What?" asks Mom.

Owen steers her on.

"Hi," says the guy who works in the reptile house. "That's a nice crocodile you've got there."

"This is not a crocodile," says Owen.

"What is it, then?" the guy asks, and laughs. "I think you'd better leave it here."

"Let go!" yells Owen. "This is my mom!"

Owen and Mom run for the exit.

"Stupid man!" yells Mom.

"Let's forget about the tigers," says Owen, panting.

Back on the street, they hear shouting and laughter coming from the playground. It's a happening place. Owen has forgotten about the hospital. He wants to try the swings. But two tough girls get there first. Mom blows a cloud of sand on them.

"Hey, cut that out!" they say, spitting and coughing.

But Mom thinks it's funny when people get sand in their eyes. She laughs with a rumble that sounds like thunder.

　　"You're scaring the little boys," says Owen.

　　"You can't stay here."

Owen takes Mom to the ice cream truck on the other side of the park. He orders two cones. Mom has forgotten how to buy things. Owen pays with a twenty-dollar bill and feels pretty cool. Owen's ice cream is delicious. But dragons think ice cream is disgusting. So Owen eats both ice cream cones. Mom finds something to eat in the grass instead.

"Try it," she says, chewing loudly.

"No way," says Owen, and takes a last lick of ice cream.

That's when Kato comes rushing up. Owen doesn't like dogs, and Kato is the most dangerous dog of all.

But Mom grabs hold of Kato. It looks as if she is going to eat him.

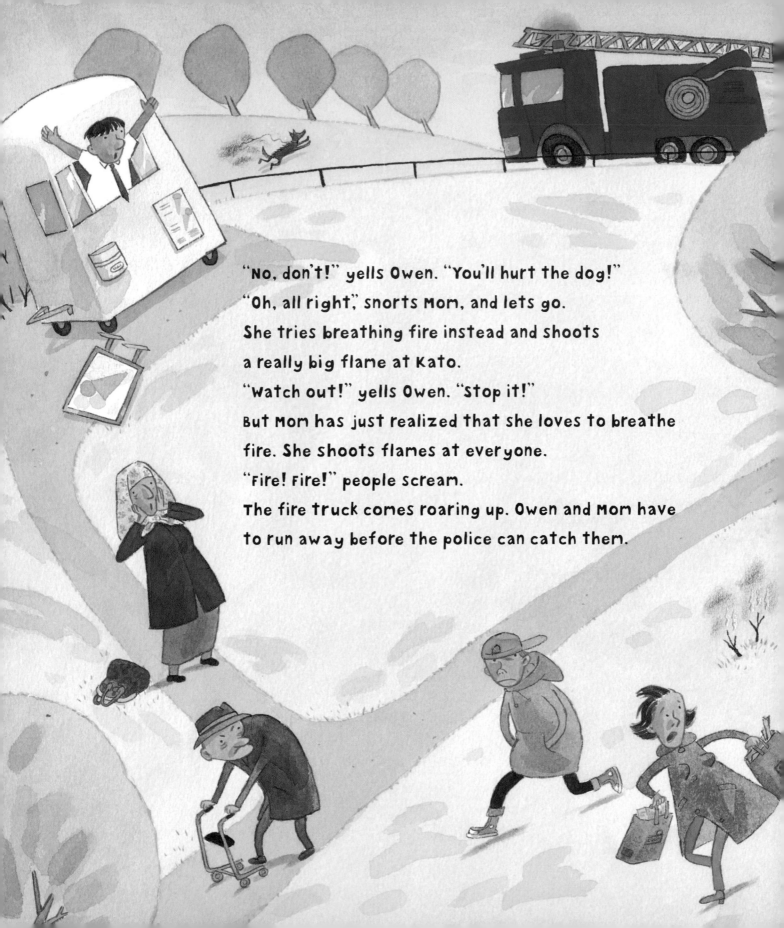

"No, don't!" yells Owen. "You'll hurt the dog!"

"Oh, all right," snorts Mom, and lets go.

She tries breathing fire instead and shoots
a really big flame at Kato.

"Watch out!" yells Owen. "Stop it!"

But Mom has just realized that she loves to breathe
fire. She shoots flames at everyone.

"Fire! Fire!" people scream.

The fire truck comes roaring up. Owen and Mom have
to run away before the police can catch them.

When they finally stop running, they are standing in front
of the gas station. That's when Owen has a brilliant idea.
He finds the glass cabinet with the air pump and cleaning
stuff and fills a large bucket with water. Then he tricks
Mom into drinking all the water!
"Now you'll never be able to breathe fire again," he says.
Mom sobs for a while, but eventually she stops.
And they continue on their way to the hospital.

They go right in to see a doctor.
"She needs a little shot," says Owen. "She has forgotten
how to do everything."
"I see," says the doctor.

"And she eats bugs and stuff like that," Owen continues.

"Too bad, we don't have an injection for that. Thank you, this visit will be one hundred bucks," says the doctor.

Mom thumps her tail angrily on the floor, and the doctor looks startled.

"Oh, I meant to say there's no charge at all," she squeaks.

"What should we do now?" asks Mom.

"I want to go home," says Owen. Running around has
actually made him quite tired.

On the way home, they stop by Grandma's.

"Why, it's Owen, Grandma's sweetheart," says Grandma.
Then she looks at Mom.

"She was like this when we woke up this morning," says Owen.

"It'll probably wear off in a few days," Grandma says, and
brings out tea and curry.

When Owen finishes eating, he's totally exhausted.
Mom has to carry him all the way home.

"Sleep tight, little one," she whispers, and puts Owen to sleep
in her own big bed.

When Owen wakes up the next morning, Mom is already up.
He hears noises from the kitchen.
Then he hears Mom talking on the phone.
"Hi, this is Bea. I've decided to take today off. I'm spending
the day with Owen."

Owen peeks out into the kitchen. His usual mom is sitting there.
But she's not in a hurry.
"Good morning, sweetie. Do you want some
chocolate milk?" she asks.

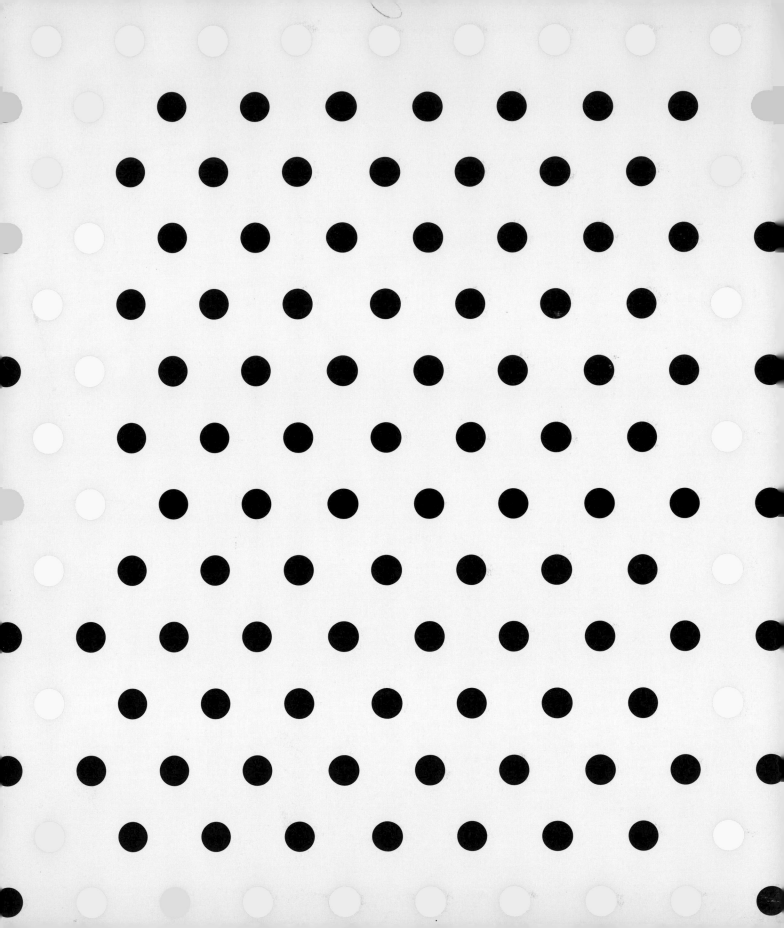